Rhys and

Meinir Wyn Edwards
Illustrated by Gini Wade

This is a story about a boy and a girl called Rhys and Meinir. They lived in a little village called Porth y Nant on the Llŷn Peninsula. The story happened about two hundred years ago, when the area was very remote and isolated. There were only three farms in the Nant at the time – Tŷ Uchaf, Tŷ Canol and Tŷ Hen. Rhys lived on one of the farms and Meinir in one of the others. They were both the same age and were best friends.

Rhys was a tall, strong boy, with a mop of black, curly hair. He lived with his two older sisters, Gwyneth and Gwen. He loved to take his sheepdog, Cidwm, for long walks and sometimes Meinir would join them. The three would walk for hours on end, but nobody ever worried about them. They knew the Nant inside out and they used to play outdoors whenever they could. They were always running down to the seashore, climbing Carreg y Llam to look at the waves crashing on the rocks below, or taking shelter under the hollow oak tree.

Meinir lived with her elderly father, Ifan Meredydd. He adored his beautiful young daughter. Rhys was a frequent visitor at their house and he often helped Ifan Meredydd on the farm. Ifan also loved Rhys and treated him like a son. He used to tease the two friends and joke that one day they would get married.

"Dad!" Meinir would say, her cheeks red. "Don't be silly. I'm only ten years old!"

And Rhys would answer,

"No way, Ifan Meredydd! Who'd want to marry someone like her!?"

And the three would laugh.

The children would never have guessed, but Ifan *had* been secretly wishing that they would marry. As the two got older, it became obvious that they were madly in love with each other.

One summer's day, when they were both about fifteen years old, they went for a walk. Rhys ran ahead towards the hollow oak tree that had been split open by bolts of lightning over the centuries. He shouted,

"Meinir, stay there! Don't come any nearer till I'm ready. Close your eyes. I've got a surprise for you!"

She shut her eyes tightly and when Rhys called, "OK, I'm ready. Come and see...", she ran towards him. He was grinning like a Cheshire cat and was pointing at the bark of the tree.

Rhys had been busy carving a heart with Rh xx M inside.

"Well? What do you think?" he asked proudly.

"Rhys! You know I love you, but you shouldn't have done that! It's unlucky," she said unhappily.

"But why? I want the world to know how much I love you. How can that be unlucky?" Rhys was very disappointed with her reaction.

"I'm sorry, Rhys," Meinir said. "But I've got a funny feeling that something's not right...", and she walked away with a sad, dreamy look on her face.

Rh + M

Years passed, and the time came at last for Rhys and Meinir to announce their wedding. The invitations were sent, the dress was made, the cake was baked and the feast was prepared. Everyone in the Nant knew the happy couple and they were all excited about the big day – Saturday, the fifth of July.

When July finally arrived, Rhys and Meinir were so excited and were rushing about trying to get everything organized. There was so much to do! Clynnog Church was filled with the scents and colours of summer flowers and it had never looked so wonderful. It was a tradition that the neighbours, on the eve of the wedding, went to the bride's house bearing gifts of good luck. So on the fourth of July, Rhys and Meinir received all kinds of presents, such as thick woollen blankets, cheese and honey. The following day would be unforgettable ...

When the morning mist cleared, the sun shone above Nant Gwrtheyrn and the sky turned bright blue. Perfect weather for the perfect wedding! There wouldn't be any confetti-throwing, but the children had been laying flowers and branches on the path leading up to the church. There wouldn't be a grand limo taking the bride to church, but Rhys's friends would escort Meinir to the wedding safely and on time.

"Please be there promptly at two o'clock tomorrow," Rhys had said. "Don't keep me waiting for too long!"

"Don't worry," Meinir said. "I'll make sure that the boys will be able to find me. Tomorrow will be the best day of my life."

And they said goodbye.

After putting on her beautiful white dress and plaiting flowers in her long hair, Meinir went to hide from the boys inside the hollow oak tree near Carreg y Llam.

The boys went to the farm to fetch her, but Ifan Meredydd told them that she had already gone to hide. The bride always went to hide on the morning of her wedding day.

They searched in the outbuildings, but she wasn't there. They ran to the woods and looked up and down every single tree, but she wasn't there either.

While they searched high and low, they shouted out her name,

"Meinir! It's nearly two o'clock."

"Come on, Meinir! Rhys will be worried."

"Where are you?"

"Please answer, Meinir!"

But there was no sign of her anywhere. Some boys ran to the church to see if she had given up on them and had decided to walk there by herself. But no. By the time they got to church, Rhys had left. It had become too late to hold the wedding that day, so he had set out to look for her.

What on earth had happened to Meinir?

Rhys frantically searched far and wide, but it was no good. All the wedding guests went home with long faces. Nothing like this had ever happened in the Nant.

As the years went by, Rhys went mad. His hair and beard grew long and he wouldn't eat or sleep for days on end. He was often seen in the woods late at night, or wandering down to Carreg y Llam where he would shout angrily at the waves. His heart had been broken.

One day, Rhys was lying by the hollow oak tree in his ragged clothes when it started to rain. The rain poured down, getting heavier and heavier by the minute, and the sky filled with thick black clouds. Rhys heard the roaring of thunder getting nearer and nearer. He was soaked to the skin, but he didn't care.

The storm got closer and white lightning tore the black sky in two. Rhys got up and screamed as loud as he could. It was as if he wanted to scream louder than the storm itself. Suddenly, there was a terrific crash behind him. The hollow oak tree had been struck by lightning once again. His eyes sparked wildly as he looked at the scene behind him. Surely...it couldn't be...

"Meinir?!"

He ran as fast as a bullet towards the tree.

"Meinir! Is that you?"

The tree had been split down the middle and there, inside the hollow oak tree was a skeleton wearing a white wedding dress. The flowers that had been plaited in Meinir's hair on her wedding day were dangling limply across the skull like a horrible crown.

Rhys fell to his knees, tears rolling down his face. As he stretched out his arm to touch his bride, lightning struck him across his back and he was killed on the spot.

He was found the following morning lying dead near the hollow oak tree, but he had a smile on his face. He died a happy man because he had, at last, found the love of his life.

The two were buried together in the cemetery at Clynnog Church. Rhys and Meinir would be together now, forever.

Welsh Folk Tales in a Flash!

5 folk tales from Wales, for all ages!
£1.95

Rhys and Meinir
Cantre'r Gwaelod
Dic Penderyn
Red Bandits of Mawddwy
Maelgwn, King of Gwynedd

Also available:

Cyfres Chwedlau Chwim

5 o hen chwedlau a straeon gwerin Cymreig i blant o bob oed!
£1.95 yr un.

Rhys a Meinir
Cantre'r Gwaelod
Dic Penderyn
Gwylliaid Cochion Mawddwy
Maelgwn Gwynedd